This book belongs to:

_____

Happy Heartwood Day

Miss Spider's
Happy Heartwood Day

David Kirk

CALLAWAY

NEW YORK

2008

The wind was whipping through Sunny Patch, so Miss Spider kept her children safe inside the Cozy Hole.

"Mom, Dragon won't let me play with his drag-glider!" Squirt yelled.

"'Cause it's mine!" Dragon bellowed.

All of a sudden, the Cozy Hole seemed smaller.

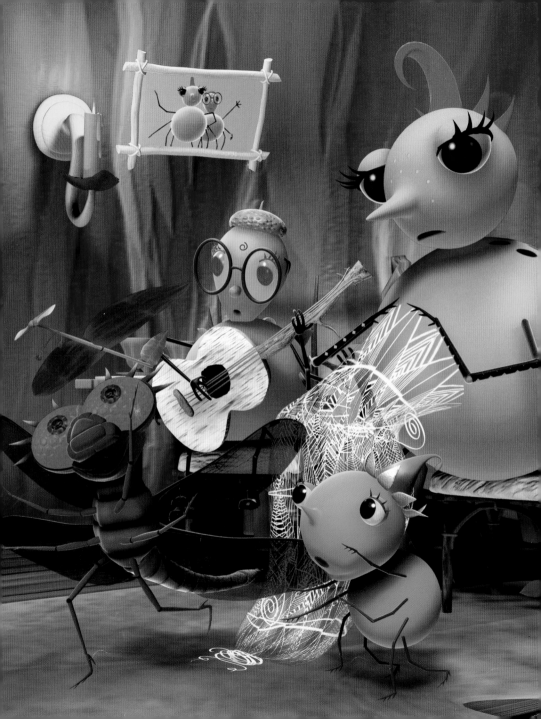

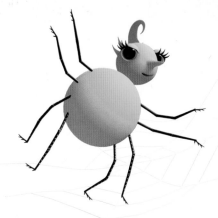

O ver the howling wind, they heard a snapping and cracking. Then, a great crash shook Sunny Patch.

As soon as the wind died down, the family went outside to investigate.

All the villagers gathered around a dead tree that had fallen in the meadow.

"Happy Heartwood Day!" laughed Miss Spider and Holley, bumping their noses.

Dragon clung to his drag-glider. "What's Heartwood Day?" he asked.

"When a tree falls in Sunny Patch, we celebrate," explained Mr. Mantis.

"It reminds us that life is precious," Miss Spider smiled, "and that we should share what we have with others. So, come on, gang—let's get ready for the Heartwood Day party!"

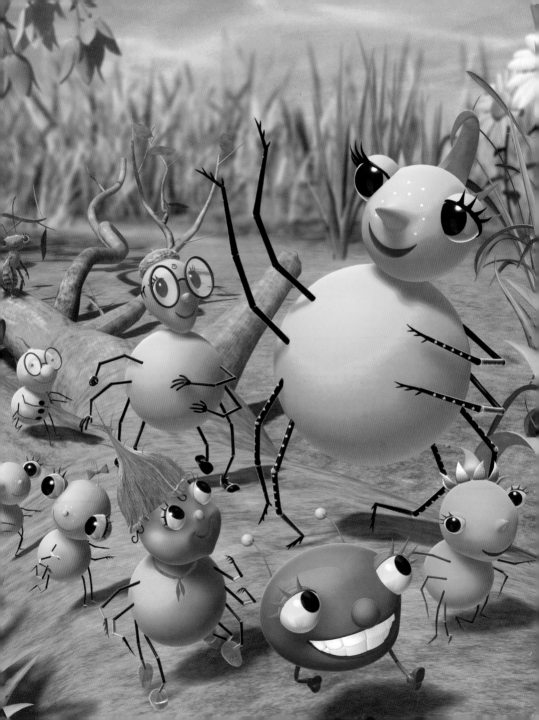

Back at the Cozy Hole, Miss Spider baked a special soufflé. "It's my puffiest ever!" she beamed.

Everybuggy made a special gift to exchange at the party—everybuggy except for Dragon. He was much too busy flying his drag-glider.

"I want a turn, too!" Squirt said, snatching it out of the air.

Dragon and Squirt wrestled for the drag-glider. The table shook until . . .

M

iss Spider's soufflé went *kaflooey*. It was ruined!

"He did it!" cried Dragon.

"No, *he* did it!" shouted Squirt.

"I wish you two would share," Miss Spider said sadly.

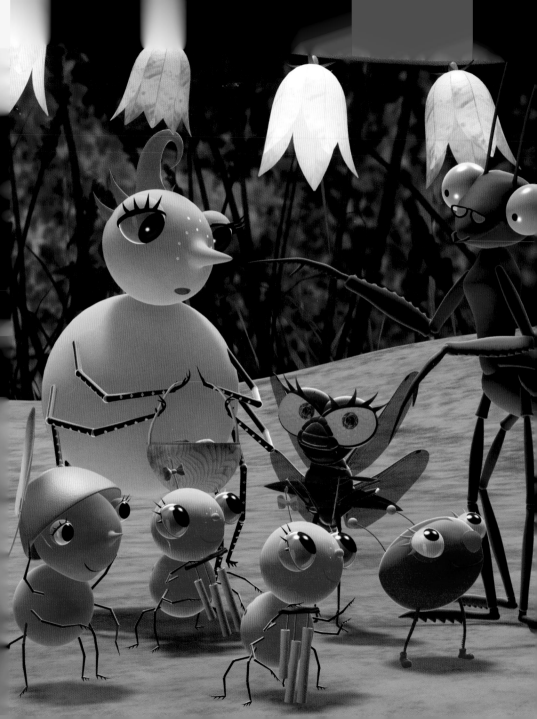

T

hen the buggy bunch left for the meadow.

"How nice, Dragon," said Mr. Mantis, greeting them as they arrived at the party. "You brought a drag-glider to exchange in the share line!"

"This is *mine*," Dragon snorted. "I don't want to share!"

"Hi, Dragon," said Snack, handing him a heart-shaped card. "I made this for you."

"Gee, thanks, Snack," he replied. "But I didn't bring anything for you."

Dragon felt a little funny.

Katy Katydid and the Cricket Band started to play a happy tune.

"Time for the share line!" announced Mr. Mantis.

Dragon looked around as everybuggy got ready to exchange their gifts.

"Don't you want to join us?"
Miss Spider asked Dragon.

"I didn't bring anything to share,"
Dragon replied sadly. "Now I wish
I had."

Dragon was walking away from
the party when he had an idea. He
ran to the share line.

"This is for you," Dragon said, handing Squirt his drag-glider.

"But it's your favorite!" Squirt exclaimed.

"Maybe you can share it with me sometime," Dragon smiled.

Katy and the Cricket Band played a Heartwood Day song, as all the bugs danced together under the glowing moon.

This book is based on the TV episode "Happy Heartwood Day," written by Alice Prodanou,
from the animated TV series *Miss Spider's Sunny Patch Friends* on Nick Jr.,
a Nelvana Limited/Absolute Pictures Limited co-production in association
with Callaway Arts & Entertainment, based on the Miss Spider books by David Kirk.

ISBN 978-0-448-45027-8   10 9 8 7 6 5 4 3 2 1

ABOUT DAVID KIRK

Master artist and storyteller David Kirk is hailed as one of today's most innovative and exciting creators of books and toys for children. Before his remarkable success in the world of children's publishing, Kirk was the founder and designer of two toy companies. His bright, hand-painted wooden toys are, together with his paintings and hand-crafted furniture, treasured by collectors and featured in books, art galleries, and museums.

Then along came a spider: Miss Spider. Inspired by his daughter Violet's love for insects in the family garden, Kirk found the perfect subject for his story. *Miss Spider's Tea Party,* a lush counting book in verse with mesmerizing oil illustrations and an important message about tolerance, quickly became a phenomenon, earning praise from booksellers and librarians across the country. Kirk followed this success by continuing the saga of Miss Spider in *Miss Spider's Wedding, Miss Spider's New Car,* and *Miss Spider's ABC.*

In addition to creating splendid books and paintings, Mr. Kirk finds time to develop his many other projects, including designing Sunny Patch, a collection of children's lifestyle products, for Target stores. He is also executive producer of *Miss Spider's Sunny Patch Friends,* a 3-D computer-animated television series on Nick Jr. The success of the series inspired a line of trade and mass-market books published by Callaway Arts & Entertainment and Penguin Young Readers Group.

Mr. Kirk lives in upstate New York with his wife, Kathy, and daughters, Violet, Primrose, and Wisteria.